EZ SPR

D1401057

SpongeBob SquarePants

LEGENDS OF BIKINI BOTTOM

as told by
ANONYMOUS
SEA-DWELLERS

illustrated by
DAVE AIKINS

SIMON SPOTLIGHT/NICKELODEON

New York   London   Toronto   Sydney

Stephen Hillenburg

Based on the TV series *SpongeBob SquarePants*™ created by Stephen Hillenburg as seen on Nickelodeon™

Book text based on the following screenplays: "Trenchbillies" and "The Curse of the Hex" written by Aaron Springer & Richard Pursel; "Welcome to the Bikini Bottom Triangle" written by Luke Brookshier, Nate Cash & Dani Michaeli; "The Main Drain" written by Luke Brookshier, Nate Cash & Doug Lawrence; "The Monster Who Came to Bikini Bottom" written by Aaron Springer & Dani Michaeli; and "Sponge-Cano" written by Casey Alexander, Zeus Cervas & Derek Iversen

SIMON SPOTLIGHT/NICKELODEON

An imprint of Simon & Schuster Children's Publishing Division

1230 Avenue of the Americas, New York, New York 10020

For information about special discounts for bulk purchases, please contact Simon & Schuster Special Sales at 1-866-506-1949 or business@simonandschuster.com.

Manufactured in the United States of America 1210 LAK

First Edition 10 9 8 7 6 5 4 3 2 1

ISBN 978-1-4424-1340-5

Far below the calm blue waters of the ocean lie many dark legends.
The mere whisper of the word trenchbilly, a passing thought about the main
drain, or the smallest suggestion of the Bikini Bottom Triangle would send chills
down the spines of even the hardiest of sea creatures! No one dared to uncover
these hidden mysteries. That is, until now . . . for none of those creatures
could hold a candle to the bravest, yellowest sponge in the whole sea. And so
SpongeBob SquarePants set off to uncover the six greatest legends of Bikini
Bottom!

LEGEND #1: The Monster Who Came to Bikini Bottom

Patrick was playing in the ocean when he met a giant monster. Most people would have been terrified, but not Patrick! He and the monster became friends. They played with a snow globe and spent the afternoon laughing together.

Patrick brought the monster to meet SpongeBob. At first SpongeBob thought the monster was hurting Patrick.

This is even worse than yesterday when the ice machine broke at the Krusty Krab, thought SpongeBob. But then he realized that the monster was Patrick's new friend.

"And you are?" SpongeBob asked.

"Rarg!" the monster roared.

"Nice to meet you, Rarg!" SpongeBob replied.

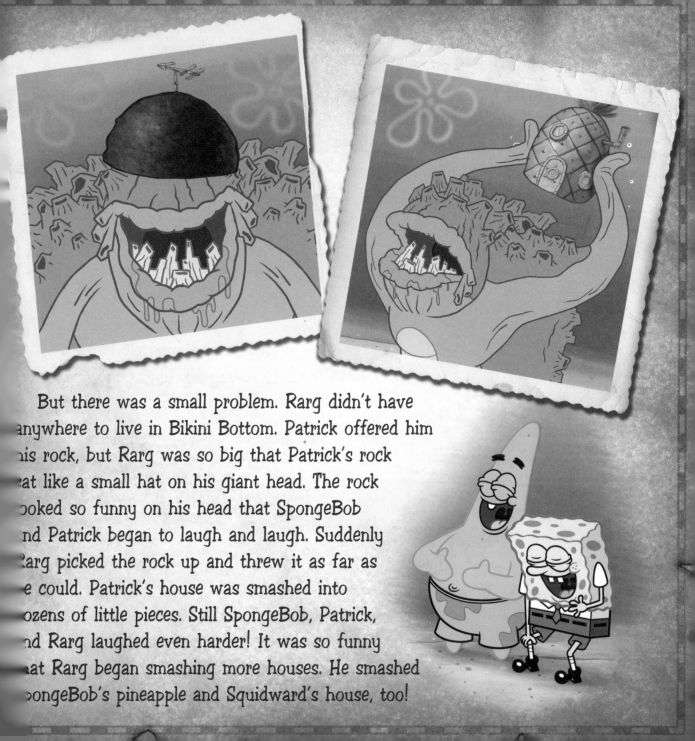

But there was a small problem. Rarg didn't have anywhere to live in Bikini Bottom. Patrick offered him his rock, but Rarg was so big that Patrick's rock sat like a small hat on his giant head. The rock looked so funny on his head that SpongeBob and Patrick began to laugh and laugh. Suddenly Rarg picked the rock up and threw it as far as he could. Patrick's house was smashed into dozens of little pieces. Still SpongeBob, Patrick, and Rarg laughed even harder! It was so funny that Rarg began smashing more houses. He smashed SpongeBob's pineapple and Squidward's house, too!

Suddenly the police came to see what all the ruckus was about. When they saw Rarg, they built a fence around him to keep him in. But Rarg was too big for the fence. He just stepped right over it and started to run! The police chased him through the streets of Bikini Bottom, and just when they had him cornered, Patrick appeared.

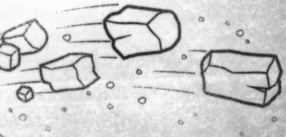

"Wait just one minute!" Patrick cried. "He's my friend. Let me talk to him first."

Patrick and Rarg came up with a plan. Rarg now lives at the top of Biki Bottom Alps and has a job. He supplie Bikini Bottom with all of their ice!

LEGEND #2: Welcome to the Bikini Bottom Triangle

Not too long ago strange things started happening in Bikini Bottom: SpongeBob's alarm clock went missing! So did Gary's shell, Squidward's clarinet, Patrick's cuff links—and even Mr. Krabs!

A sailor told them that legend says when an eerie fog rolls in, and the song of the mermaids is heard, things disappear into the Bikini Bottom Triangle—and they never come back! SpongeBob and Squidward searched high and low for Mr. Krabs when a fog rolled in, and mermaids began to sing. . . .

Suddenly Squidward and SpongeBob were sucked into a chute. They landed on a giant pile of discarded things—a gum-ball machine, a fridge, some tennis rackets, and even lawn mowers! A few moments later Patrick and Pearl came tumbling through the chute too.

Soon they found Mr. Krabs. He was having the time of his life. In fact he wanted to stay in the Bikini Bottom Triangle—until he thought that Plankton might be running the Krusty Krab!

SpongeBob and Patrick asked the singing mermaids for help.

"Look, we only know one thing. Nothing ever leaves the Bikini Bottom Triangle," they answered. "That's how we surround ourselves with cool new stuff. Anything beyond that is T.N.O.P.: totally not our problem."

They didn't care that SpongeBob and his friends were stuck.

But then Pearl told them that the mall had the best, coolest, most glitterishly fabulous new stuff. Now the mermaids wanted to go to the mall!

SpongeBob had an idea: If the mermaids sang their song backward, it might reverse the direction of the giant chute.

Instead of sucking things into the triangle, it would shoot everything inside back out.

It worked! Pearl and the mermaids immediately headed for the mall. And SpongeBob and Mr. Krabs discovered that the mysterious saild had kept the Krusty Krab running the whole time they were gone!

"You've got a little vermin problem," said the sailor.

LEGEND 3: The Curse of the Hex

One dark and stormy night an old hagfish appeared at the Krusty Krab just as Squidward was locking up. She forced her way in, but Squidward refused to take her order. She just kept begging for a Krabby Patty, and Squidward and Mr. Krabs couldn't get her to leave. Then SpongeBob walked over to her and whispered something in her ear.

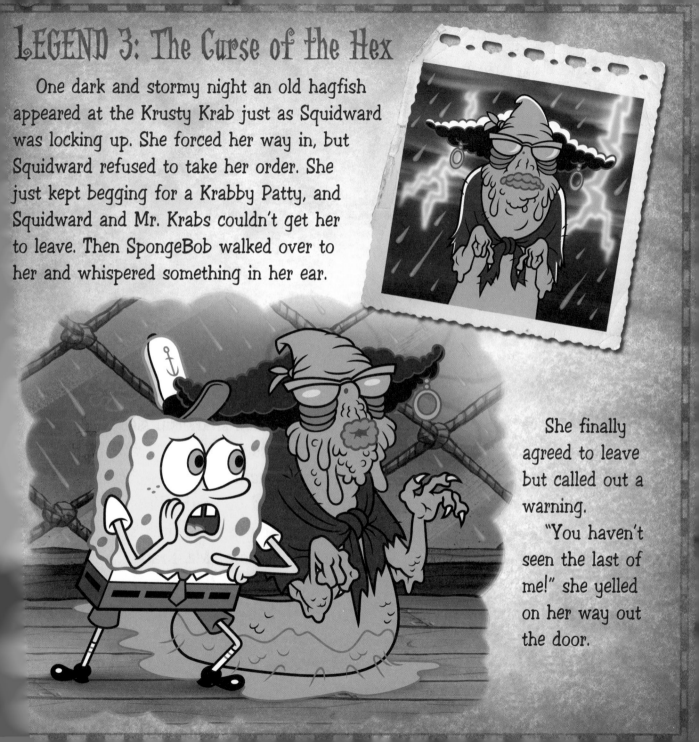

She finally agreed to leave but called out a warning.

"You haven't seen the last of me!" she yelled on her way out the door.

Later SpongeBob
sneaked out of the Krusty
Krab with two Krabby
Patties for the hagfish.
But as SpongeBob handed
her the Patties, Mr. Krabs
showed up and grabbed
them first!

Angered, the hagfish
shouted, "Eye of newt and
frozen sharkskin slab, I hereby
curse the Krusty Krab!"
The next day no customers
showed up at the Krusty Krab,
and a mysterious fire
burned some of Mr. Krabs'
hard-earned cash! So he
set off with SpongeBob
to beg and plead with the
hagfish to remove her
awful curse!

The hagfish said she would lift the curse if they brought her the sacred gold doubloon from the throat of the giant golden eel. So SpongeBob led the way and retrieved the gold doubloon. The hagfish promptly used the coin for laundry. "Finally!" she said.

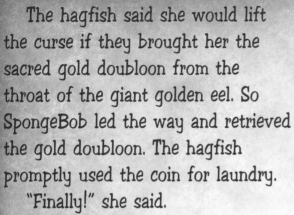

Then they went to the Krusty Krab, and the hagfish pulled out a wooden CLOSED sign from in front of the restaurant. It wasn't a curse after all! Relieved, Mr. Krabs and SpongeBob returned to work.

LEGEND 4: The Main Drain

Mr. Krabs once told SpongeBob and Patrick a scary story—the story of the main drain!

Mr. Krabs told them how two little boys many years ago stumbled upon a giant plug at the center of the ocean. They didn't know what it was, so they pulled on it. Suddenly everything was being sucked into the hole! Not only did the two kids go down the drain, but so did all of the houses and people of Bikini Bottom!

SpongeBob and Patrick decided to trek across the ocean to find the main drain to protect it. But when they got there, Patrick did not believe it was the real thing. They were about to pull the plug to make sure it was real when Mr. Krabs and Plankton showed up.

Mr. Krabs confessed that he and Plankton were the two kids in the story he told them, and he begged them not to pull the plug.

But Patrick accidentally pulled and they were all sucked into he drain . . . along with all of ikini Bottom!

Luckily, it was just a bedtime story!

LEGEND #5: Trenchbillies

One day SpongeBob and Patrick were chasing a jellyfish when they fell off a cliff down, down, down, until finally, they landed. *Hard.* Right on top of a trenchbilly! The trenchbilly dragged them to the leader, Ma Angler.

"As leader of this clan," she growled, "I must subject you to our clan initiation rites to see if you're worthy . . . of living!"

A trenchbilly walked up to them with his fiddle in hand, and he played a song. "SpongeBob, I think it's meant to be a musical challenge," Patrick whispered.

So SpongeBob grabbed a pair of suspenders and fastened them to his pants. Then Patrick picked up SpongeBob and began to strum on his suspenders like a guitar!

They passed the challenge—phew!

Next it was time for the hootin' and hollerin' contest. The trenchbillies' best singer, Betsy, yodeled the loudest, strongest yodel she could muster.

"What are we going to do?" SpongeBob asked.

"I don't know," Patrick answered. "But I sure am thirsty!"

Patrick opened a can of corn and began gulping. SpongeBob grabbed the can and gulped down the rest. Afterward they each let out the loudest, strongest burps ever!

The crowd went *wild*!

Next they were challenged to a wrestling match. But SpongeBob and Patrick showed everyone how to jellyfish instead. At first Ma Angler wasn't impressed, but then SpongeBob and Patrick jumped high into the air, collided, and collapsed on the ground. Ma Angler thought those were great wrestling moves, and she made them honorary trenchbillies!

She gave them each a set of trenchbilly teeth. A few moments later they learned that meant they'd have to stay there and take care of her forever! Hearing that, SpongeBob and Patrick ran as fast as they could back to Bikini Bottom where they belonged!

NOVELTY TEETH

LEGEND #6: Sponge-Cano

On a beautiful sunny day in Bikini Bottom, SpongeBob felt the urge to sing about all of the things he was grateful for. He was grateful for his house, his life in Bikini Bottom, and especially for his neighbor. Except his neighbor, Squidward, wasn't so grateful for all of that singing outside his window.

In fact it distracted him so much that he tripped over his paintbrushes and ended up breaking one of the water pipes in his basement, flooding it.

"I can give you a hand, neighbor!" SpongeBob said.

"No! You've done enough already!" yelled Squidward. "I don' want your help ever again!"

Realizing he was late for his job at the Krusty Krab, Squidward quickly fixed the water pipe and ran to work. But being at work didn't exactly change Squidward's attitude. He was grumpy and rude to the customers all day.

"This day couldn't get any worse," rumbled Squidward. "I'm the most miserable person in Bikini Bottom!"

Suddenly everyone heard a loud rumbling and could see fire raining down everywhere in Bikini Bottom. Mount Bikini Bottom had just erupted!

The town was in a panic! The raining lava was burning holes in everything—even through the roof of the Krusty Krab! It looked like Bikini Bottom was doomed!

That was until an ancient warrior, who had ruled over the ocean before the dawn of time, came to tell them how to stop it.

"To stop the volcano you must sacrifice the most miserable person . . . ," said the warrior.

Before he could finish speaking, the crowd began chanting, "Squidward! Squidward!" They tied him to a stake and carried him to the volcano. They were about to throw him in when . . .

"I am grateful for the life I have! Please help me, SpongeBob!" pleaded Squidward.

"You told me not to help you ever again," said SpongeBob.

Just then they heard another loud rumbling throughout Bikini Bottom—could it be another volcano? No, it was the pipe in Squidward's house exploding from the water pressure. The water blew the house into the air, and it landed right on the volcano. Bikini Bottom was saved!

"But you said the sacrifice had to be the most miserable person!" Squidward cried.

"No one let me finish," the warrior said. "I was going to say you must sacrifice the most miserable person's house to the volcano. No one ever listens to me!"

And so our brave SpongeBob survived and lived to tell about the legends of the deep . . . but not everyone is so lucky. Some never got out of the Bikini Bottom Triangle or even became trenchbillies. But now you know and can go out to uncover more hidden mysteries. What spine-chilling creatures will you discover?